Modern Curriculum Press
BEGINNING TO READ Series

The Three Bears

The Three Bears

Margaret Hillert

illustrated by Irma Wilde

MODERN CURRICULUM PRESS
Cleveland • Toronto

ISBN 0-8136-5015-1 (hardbound)
ISBN 0-8136-5515-3 (paperback)

89 92 91 90

See the house.

It is red and yellow.

It is a funny little house.

One, two, three.

One is the father.

One is the mother.

One is the baby.

The father is big.

The baby is little.

See Mother work.

Mother can make something.

Away we go.

Away, away, away.

I can play.

My ball is blue.

See it go up.

Oh, look.

Here is a little house.

A funny little house.

I can go in.

Here is something.

Red, yellow, and blue.

One is big.

One is little.

I want something.

Here is one for me.

Here is something.

Red, yellow, and blue.

One is big.

One is little.

Here is one for me.

Here is something.

Red, yellow, and blue.

One is big.

One is little.

Here is one for me.

Here we come.

We can go in.

Father said, “Oh, oh!”

Mother said, “Oh, my!”

Baby said, “Oh, look!

It is not here.”

Father said, "Oh, oh!"

Mother said, "Oh, my!"

Baby said, "Oh, look!

It is down."

Father said, “Oh, oh!”

Mother said, “Oh, my!”

Baby said, “Oh, look!

I see something.”

Help, help!

I can jump down.

I can run.

Oh, Mother, Mother.

Here I come!

Modern Curriculum Press Beginning-To-Read Books

Margaret Hillert, author of several books in the MCP Beginning-To-Read Series, is a writer, poet, and teacher.

The Three Bears

Children will find new enjoyment in this favorite tale, beautifully illustrated, and with a text that uses 45 preprimer words.

Word List

7 see
the
house
it
is
red
and
yellow
a
funny
little

8 one
two
three
father
mother
baby

9 big

10 work
can
make
something

11 away
we
go

12 I
play
my
ball
blue
up

13 oh
look
here
in

15 want
for
me

20 come

22 said
not

23 down

25 help
run
jump